Cody Beck

Long Stretch at First Base

Long Stretch at First Base

by Matt Christopher

Illustrated by Karen Meyer

Little, Brown and Company
Boston New York Toronto London

First Paperback Edition

ISBN 0-316-14101-1
Library of Congress Catalog Card Number 60-5872

10 9 8 7 6 5 4 3

MV-NY

Published simultaneously in Canada
by Little, Brown & Company (Canada) Limited

Printed in the United States of America

Long Stretch at First Base

1

BOBBY stood in the pitcher's box in the pasture field where the kids played scrub baseball. His older brother Kirby was batting. Bobby took his windup, stretched, and threw a looping ball toward the plate. The grass-stained baseball arched like a rainbow.

Tall, dark-haired Kirby yanked his bat back upon his shoulder with disgust.

"Come on, Bobby!" he shouted. "Throw that ball faster, will you?"

"You can't hit it if I do!" Bobby cried.

Kirby's face turned red. And Bobby knew that he had said something he shouldn't have. Kirby was older and a lot taller than Bobby. He played first base for the Redbirds in the Grasshoppers League. But he was a poor hitter. He always took a hard cut at the ball, and almost always missed it.

"Oh, all right," said Bobby. "I'll throw it faster."

Catcher Dave Gessini returned the ball to Bobby. Dave was the regular catcher for the Redbirds. He was wearing his mask and chest protector. The only three other players present were in the outfield. One of them was Ann, Bobby's sister. She was in between Bobby's and Kirby's age, and liked baseball just as much as most boys did. She could throw as well as a boy, too.

Bobby wound up again, stretched, and delivered. He had a side-arm delivery. The ball raced for the plate and curved in just a little.

Kirby stepped into it, took a hard cut.

Plup! The ball landed solidly in Dave's mitt.

"Let somebody else bat for a while!" one of the boys in the outfield shouted.

"Sure! He's been up there an hour now!" the other said.

"He has not!" Bobby heard Ann say. "He needs practice just like the rest of you do!"

Bobby turned and looked at them. The boys didn't say anything back to Ann. They never did dare say much back to her. She always had a good answer for them.

Bobby pitched another straight ball over the heart of the plate. This time Kirby hit it on the ground. The ball hopped out to the outfield. One of the players fielded it and pegged it in to Bobby.

There, thought Bobby. Finally Kirby

had connected. Bobby could not understand it, though. He himself didn't have much trouble hitting the ball at all.

A boy in the outfield ran in to bat. Kirby replaced him. As Kirby ran past Bobby, Bobby saw the disappointed look on his face. Terry, their black Scottish terrier, chased and barked at Kirby's heels.

"Come on, Terry!" Bobby yelled. "Get back here!"

Terry hopped around Kirby's feet for a while, then trotted back, his inch-long tail wagging hard.

Bobby pitched to the batter. After a while he batted and another boy pitched. He pounded out three grounders and four flies to the outfield. One was a poke that would have gone for a home run in a real game.

"For a little guy you pack a lot of

power," Dave said, grinning behind his mask. "What a difference between you and Kirby!"

Bobby didn't say anything.

Ann batted next. After she hit a few, they quit practicing.

"Who do we play this afternoon?" asked Bobby, who seldom kept up with the schedule.

"The Yankee Clippers," answered Kirby, who *always* kept up with the schedule. He had on his first-base mitt, and was tossing a baseball in the air and catching it. Bobby had never seen anybody who loved baseball as much as Kirby did. He'd play every minute of the day if somebody played with him.

"They're in second place," said Dave.

"If we beat them, we'll be in second," said Kirby. "And if we win Friday, and the Seals lose, we'll be in first place."

One thing about Kirby: He knew the records of the teams, and even of the players, better than anyone.

The game with the Yankee Clippers began at six o'clock. Curt Barrows, the coach of the Redbirds, hit grounders to the infielders just before game time. Then he gave a short pep talk to his team while the Clippers had the field.

"Cappie Brennan will start pitching," Mr. Barrows said. He had a piece of paper in his hand on which was written the line-up. "Dave will catch. Kirby, you start at first base. Catch those throws and let's see you get some hits at the plate. You haven't been hitting at all. And we need hits. The Clippers are a tough bunch. The rest of the infield will be the regular starting line-up. Al Dakin at second, Bobby Jamison at short, and Mark Donahue at third. In left field is Toby Warren, in center Jim Hurwitz, and in right Jerry Echols."

The Redbirds, with their name printed in red on the front of their white jerseys, took the field first. Kirby started the chatter. It was quickly taken up by the other infielders.

"Come on, Cappie! Come on, boy! Get 'em out!"

"Whip it past 'em, Cappie!"

2

CAPPIE stepped on the mound. He was built like a young tree. His arms were like long, slender branches. He yanked on his red baseball cap and waited for the signal from Dave.

A Yankee Clipper stepped to the plate. The Clippers wore white jerseys and blue caps. He cut at the first pitch and missed.

"Strike one!" said the umpire behind the plate.

Cappie breezed another past the batter for strike two. Then he threw two straight balls. The batter cut at the next one and grounded it to Bobby at short. It was a high bouncing ball. For a moment Bobby was afraid that it might bounce over his head if he didn't get in the right spot. He ran in a little, caught the ball as it hopped up just after hitting the ground, and pegged it to first.

His heart rose to his throat. The ball was sailing wide of the base! Kirby stretched far out, the toe of his sneaker just touching the bag. The ball smacked into the hollow of his mitt an eye-winking second before the runner touched the bag!

"Out!" yelled the base umpire, throwing up a thumb.

Car horns tooted and people in the bleachers shouted their approval.

"Nice catch, Bobby!"

"Nice stretching, Kirby!"

Boy! thought Bobby. It's a good thing that Kirby's playing first base. Tony would never have caught that ball. Tony

Mandos was their other first baseman.

"One out, Cappie!" yelled Kirby, who was always the first to shout anything. "Let's get two!"

The second Yankee Clipper knocked a hot grounder to second. Al Dakin fumbled it. He picked it up finally and threw it wildly to first. Kirby stepped off the bag. By the time he caught the ball and touched the bag the runner was on.

Now the Yankee Clippers fans yelled and tooted their horns.

Cappie made his stretch and threw. *Crack!* A high fly to center field. Jim Hurwitz ran back, got under it, and plucked it out of the air. The runner on first stayed on the bag.

The next man hit a high foul ball straight above Dave Gessini's head. Dave flung off his mask, circled under the ball like a nervous tightrope walker. No one made a sound as the ball sailed as high as it could, then started coming down.

For a while it looked as though Dave wouldn't catch the ball. Then suddenly plop! He had it!

Three outs!

"Nice going, boys," Curt Barrows said as the team ran in and stumbled into the dugout. "Now for some bingles."

Bobby led off. He was the smallest man on the team and managed to get on base more often than the others. He put the protective helmet over his cap and stepped to the plate.

Tom Kohn, pitching for the Clippers, looked like a giant on the mound. He got his signal from the catcher, wound up, and delivered. He threw overhand. The ball sailed in as if from a great height.

It headed for the heart of the plate like a white rocket. Bobby swung. *Tick!* The ball fouled to the backstop screen.

The next two pitches were high. Strike one, ball two.

Then, *crack!* A line drive over third!

Bobby dropped the bat and beelined to first. He made the turn, ran to second as the left fielder picked up the ball. A two-bagger!

Bobby pulled off his protective helmet and threw it to the first-base coach. Then he stood on the bag with his hands on his knees and waited for Al Dakin to do something.

Al was a funny batter. He kept wiggling his body like a worm and moving his bat back and forth.

"Hey, Wiggles!" somebody yelled. "Let's see you hit that apple!"

Al took two strikes and then two balls. Then he hit a high fly to center. Bobby held his base as he saw the center fielder run back. For a moment he thought that the ball was going over the center fielder's head. But suddenly the player stopped, reached up his glove and picked the ball out of the air. Quickly Bobby pushed himself from the bag and tore for third. As he reached the third-base sack he saw the coach hold up both hands, which meant that he didn't have to slide.

Left fielder Toby Warren hit a blooping fly to the pitcher for the second out. Jim Hurwitz, the tall, skinny center fielder, who wore dark-rimmed glasses, took the first pitch for a called strike. Then he drove a hard grounder to third. The ball struck the third baseman's arm and glanced off to the outfield. Bobby scored.

Then Dave Gessini poled a long fly to left field. The ball was high. The Clippers outfielder got under it in plenty of time and caught it for the third out.

"All right! Hurry in, hurry out!" shouted the plate umpire.

The second inning went scoreless for both sides. In the third, the Yankee Clippers lead-off man singled through short. A triple over the head of right fielder Jerry Echols scored him. 1–1.

Cappie bore down. He struck out the next two batters. The next Clipper walked. Now there were men on first and third.

Cappie stepped off the mound, stooped and picked up some dirt in his hand. He rubbed it between his fingers a little and then let it filter back to the ground. He's nervous, Bobby thought. Every time a man reached third Cappie got nervous.

Cappie gave the batter a free ticket to fill the bases.

"All right, Cappie, boy!" Kirby shouted from first base. "Settle down! Bear down and get 'em out!"

Cappie stretched and delivered.

"Ball one!"

The chatter in the infield grew louder and louder. "C'mon, Cappie! Give 'im that sinker!"

"Ball two!"

Again Cappie backed off the mound, picked up some dirt, and dropped it.

"Strike!" A beautiful pitch over the heart of the plate.

"Thataway, Cappie!"

Then, "Strike two!"

Bobby's heart pounded. That batter was a big kid. If he connected solidly with one of Cappie's fast pitches he'd knock it over the centerfield fence and clean the bases.

Cappie stepped on the mound. He toed the rubber, stretched, threw.

Crack! A line drive to short! Bobby raised his glove. *Smack!* The ball stung the palm of his hand, but he held it.

Three outs!

"Nice catch, Bobby!" Coach Barrows said, smiling broadly. "That would have gone for two or three bases for sure!"

Bobby grinned as he sat down. "I hardly knew I had it!" he said.

Kirby patted him gently on the knee. "Beautiful catch, Bobby. I wish I could hit as good as you can catch."

"You will," said Bobby. "Just get up there and swing."

Kirby put on the protective helmet. He

waited till the Clippers pitcher threw his three practice throws to the catcher and for the umpire to yell "Play ball!" Then he walked to the plate.

Kirby swung hard at the first pitch. Strike one. He swung hard again — so hard he fell to the ground. Strike two.

"He tries to kill it," said Coach Barrows. "I've told him a hundred times not to swing too hard."

Bobby looked at Kirby and wished for a hit. A heaviness came over his heart. He just couldn't understand it — Kirby being so big and not being able to hit. At least, he was a good first baseman. *Nobody* could beat him at that position.

"Strike three!" yelled the umpire.

Kirby turned away from the plate, his eyes toward the ground. His bottom lip was curled up. He tossed the bat aside, walked to the end of the dugout and sat down.

"You're still swinging too hard," said Curt Barrows. "Swing easy. Just meet the ball."

Kirby acted as though he didn't hear.

Bobby was up next. He belted a line drive over third for two bases. Then Al stepped to the plate. He knocked a hot grounder to short. Bobby started for third – and got caught in a hot box! The Clippers shortstop and third baseman threw the ball back and forth between them as Bobby tried hard to keep from being tagged. Suddenly he slipped. The third baseman touched him with the ball.

Two away.

Toby Warren drove a single over short, sending Al to second. Then Jim Hurwitz hit a two-two pitch for a triple between left and center fields. Two runs crossed the plate. Dave Gessini grounded out to end the inning.

Score: Redbirds – 3, Yankee Clippers – 1.

In the top of the fourth the Clippers scored twice, tying the score. The Redbirds got two men on base at their turn at bat, Cappie and Dick Carachi. Dick was replacing Jerry in right field. The batter was Kirby.

I hope he hits, Bobby said to himself. He can break the score, and perhaps win the game. He'll feel awful good if he does.

Kirby hit the ball all right – but directly into the pitcher's hands. Bobby flied out to left, ending the inning.

The Clippers came to bat, sparkling with the hope to pile up a lot of runs.

They pushed one across to break the tie and go into the lead, 4–3.

The Redbirds failed to get a man on base.

In the sixth and final inning the Clippers were held scoreless. The Redbirds, trailing by one run, came to bat with their last chance looking slimmer than a lizard's tail. Don Robinson, batting for Dave, knocked out a single, followed by a single by Mark Donahue. Cappie flied out. Dick blasted a line drive directly at the shortstop. The shortstop caught the ball, doubled up Don, who didn't tag up in time, and the game was over.

"Well," said Dave, as he rode home with Bobby and Kirby in Mr. Jamison's car, "guess we stay in third place."

"Or maybe we dropped to fourth," said

Kirby. He shook his head sadly. "Boy, that ball looks so easy to hit."

"You swing too hard," his father said. "You're trying to hit home runs."

"That's what Mr. Barrows told me," Kirby said. "Guess I just don't know how."

Bobby looked at him, then looked away. Kirby loved baseball a lot more than he ever would. Why hadn't Kirby gotten those hits instead of him? It wouldn't have bothered *him* if he hadn't gotten any. Guess that was something he would never figure out.

That night at the supper table Mrs. Jamison acted all put out about the beans and the lettuce in their garden.

"Something's been eating them," she said. "I don't know what it is, but I think we should do something or all our work will go for nothing."

"We'll camp up there under the trees tonight, Mom," suggested Kirby. "Maybe we can find out what it is."

"Oh, boy!" cried Bobby. "That'll be fun! Maybe it's a skunk or something."

"More likely a woodchuck," said Mr. Jamison.

Just before dark Bobby and Kirby put up their tent under the trees that grew along one edge of their large vegetable garden. Ann helped them to hold up the center poles while they drove in the stakes. Then Kirby and Bobby dug a shallow ditch around the tent in case of rain.

That night they slept in their sleeping bags. They listened to the *crick! crick! crick!* of crickets, and talked about baseball until Bobby got sleepy and didn't want to talk any more.

Suddenly he awoke. Somebody was pushing his shoulder. He rose on his elbow, blinked open his eyes.

"Bobby! Come here, quick! Look what's out there!"

Kirby's excited voice took all the sleepiness out of Bobby. He crawled to the opening of the tent. Kirby held the flap open while they both looked out.

Against the moonlit darkness a shadow was moving in the garden. A big shadow — even bigger than a man.

3

BOBBY trembled. He was scared. He took hold of Kirby's pajamas and clung to them tightly.

"What – what is it, Kirby?" he whispered tensely.

"I don't know!" Kirby whispered back. "But it doesn't look like a man, unless he's a giant!"

"It can't be a giant, could it, Kirby?"

"Nah. There aren't any giants. Except in circuses."

Bobby was glad that Kirby was beside him. Kirby didn't seem scared at all. He would know what to do.

Kirby pulled the flap open wider and began to crawl out.

"Where are you going?" asked Bobby breathlessly.

"I'm going to get closer to that thing – whatever it is," replied Kirby. "It can't see us. It's dark. Just don't make a noise."

"You *sure* you want to go out there?" said Bobby worriedly.

"That's what we're here for, isn't it? To find out what's eating Mom's beans?"

"Think it's an animal?"

"What else could it be?" said Kirby. "Okay. Quit talking now. If you're too scared to come with me, stay inside the tent."

Bobby wet his lips. "I'll come," he said.

They crawled out of the tent on their hands and knees. Bobby stayed as close as possible to Kirby and tried not to make any noise.

The big, dark object was about fifty

feet away. Bobby could hear a soft, snipping sound coming from it, but he couldn't make out what it was. As they got closer the strange noise grew louder. It sounded like the tearing of leaves, followed by a steady *crunch, crunch!*

Gradually the big shadow took shape against the velvet sky. Bobby could make out the body of something shaped like a horse. Only it wasn't a horse, because the legs were too thin.

And then the animal raised its head and Bobby and Kirby stood stock-still and held their breaths in deep silence. On the head of the animal were antlers. They weren't big, but there must have been six or eight points altogether. For a moment Bobby forgot being scared, and thought that this true-life picture was the most beautiful he had ever seen.

"It's a deer!" cried Kirby softly.

The deer whirled its head toward the boys. The moonlight flashed against its big, saucer-wide eyes. Then it spun and bounded across the field, its short, white-tipped tail bobbing like a flag behind it.

The boys stood up. They watched it run. But the deer was soon out of sight behind the cherry trees and young oak saplings that grew beyond the edge of the garden.

"Well! So he's the critter who's been eating our beans!" exclaimed Kirby. "Bet he won't come back here again!"

Bobby heaved a sigh and smiled. "Boy! Wasn't he beautiful?"

"Sure was," said Kirby. "I never dreamed it was a deer."

"Me, either," said Bobby. "Well, let's

get back to our tent. But I don't think I'll sleep any more tonight."

They went back to the tent. Under the warm cover of the sleeping bag, Bobby said, "You weren't scared at all, were you, Kirby?"

Kirby chuckled. "Not exactly scared. I just didn't know what that thing was. I figured it must have been an animal, though. That's all it could have been."

Bobby smiled in the darkness. He was sure glad that he had Kirby for a brother. Kirby wasn't afraid of anything. But it was funny that he couldn't hit a baseball.

Later that night Bobby awakened again with a start. There was a steady patter against the tent. And the quiet night had turned into one filled with noises. The heavens snapped and boomed like giant firecrackers. Lightning lit up the night for a brief instant, and then thunder rolled across the sky.

Bobby shook with fright. He snuggled tighter under the covers.

"Bobby, are you awake?" Kirby's voice came softly through the gloom.

It was pitch dark inside the tent, now. The heavy rain clouds had covered the moon and put a black curtain over the night.

"Yes." Bobby felt better at once.

"You want to come in here with me?"

Bobby raised his head. "Is there room in there for both of us?"

"Sure, there is."

Bobby thought a moment. Then he laid his head back down. "No, never mind. I can sleep better separate."

"Okay," said Kirby.

Bobby listened to the whip-like cracks of thunder, and imagined covered wagons rolling their way across a rugged, rocky trail like those he had read about in books and seen on television. He saw the flashes of lightning, and remembered a spotlight at an airport that he had once seen lighting up the night just like that. He listened to the rain. After a while his eyes grew heavy again. Pretty soon he didn't hear the noises any more.

The next time Bobby opened his eyes he saw daylight through the canvas tent. He saw the slanting sides of the tent ripple like waves on a pool of water, and heard the rustle of leaves which meant that the wind was blowing. Birds chirped as though they were happy the rainy night was over.

He looked at Kirby. Kirby was still asleep. Bobby smiled. He rolled over on his back and went on listening to the noises.

After a while Kirby awoke. "Hi!" he said. "Oh, boy! It stopped raining! Come on! Let's get dressed and tell Mom and Dad what we saw last night."

They dressed quickly and ran down to the house. Terry hopped out of his dog-house, his short tail wagging fiercely. He strained at the end of the rope that held him and barked at the boys.

"Morning, Terry!" Bobby and Kirby greeted him. They both held him a few moments, then ran into the house.

"We saw what it was that was eating our beans and lettuce, Mom!" Kirby cried excitedly. "You'd never guess!"

"A woodchuck," Mrs. Jamison guessed. Her cheeks dimpled with a smile.

"Nope," said Bobby. "It was a deer."

"A deer?" Mrs. Jamison's brows lifted in surprise. "I would never have guessed!"

The boys told her all about their experience with the deer, and then about the heavy rain.

"I heard the rain, too," said Mrs. Jamison softly. "I was worried about you."

Bobby grinned proudly. "You don't have to worry about us, Mom," he said.

Ann came into the kitchen while they were eating their cereal. They told her all about their experience, too.

She said, "I'm glad I wasn't out there. Not in *that* rain!"

Bobby laughed. "We were inside the tent. And we had a ditch around it so that the water couldn't come in. It was impossible to get wet."

After breakfast, Kirby went to his room and closed the door. Soon the notes of a saxophone boomed softly, and Bobby knew where Kirby would be for the next half-hour.

4

BOBBY got a pint jar with a metal cover from the basement, and went outside. He climbed up the hill near the tent and walked slowly through the rows of corn. Grasshoppers flitted through the air around him. Presently he found exactly what he was looking for — a praying mantis.

He plucked it up carefully, put it into the jar, and screwed on the lid. Then he carried it home proudly. He lifted the lid off the large glass terrarium he kept by the basement door and tipped the praying mantis gently in.

"I'll call him Manty," he said half aloud.

Bobby grinned happily as he looked at

the other things he had collected. Spiders, grasshoppers, crickets, walking sticks, butterflies, and a little toad no bigger than his thumb. He had ants, too. They were in a glass ant-house he had made with his dad's help.

Ann and Kirby thought that he was crazy collecting stuff like that, but he would rather do that than play baseball. He was a Cub Scout, and collecting insects was his favorite hobby. He had fun watching the insects move around and eat and do things with the dirt and leaves he had put with them.

Ann came down the steps. She sat on a chair in front of an old desk. She was wearing dungarees. A rubber band held her blond hair up in a pony tail.

"Kirby wants you to play baseball with him," she said.

Bobby frowned. "Now? I don't want to play now."

"I told him the ground must be wet. But he said it isn't."

Bobby looked at her. "I wish Kirby wasn't so crazy about baseball. It's a wonder he practices his saxophone lessons."

"How about you?" said Ann. "You're crazy about those grasshoppers and walking sticks and some of those other awful-looking things. If you ask me, I think baseball is a lot more fun than *that*."

"Not me," said Bobby. He leaned over and peered at the little toad. He tapped the glass softly and grinned. "Hi, Toady," he said.

Ann made a face. "He's cute now. But wait till he grows up!"

Bobby laughed.

Somebody pounded on the basement

door that led outside. Bobby looked and recognized Kirby through the glass window. "Bobby! Are you coming?"

Bobby started to say no, but Ann interrupted him. "Why don't you go, Bobby? He loves to have you play. He's bigger and older, but he knows that you can hit better than he can."

Bobby rolled the words around in his mind. "Isn't it funny about Kirby, Ann? Isn't it funny how he can hardly hit?"

Ann shrugged. "I guess so. Go on. He's waiting for you."

"Okay." He yelled to Kirby that he'd be right out. Then he took one last look at the terrarium, went upstairs and got his glove.

Kirby and Bobby walked to the field. They had to walk down the macadam road a short distance to get to it. The regular baseball diamond was in the opposite direction. It was beyond the creek, about a mile and a half away.

Terry tagged along at their heels. Ann went, too. She had Kirby's old glove. Kirby had a brand-new first-base mitt. It was made differently than Tony Mandos's mitt. Tony's had a large leather web between the thumb and first finger.

Several boys were already at the field: Dave Gessini with his catcher's equipment, Al Dakin, Jerry Echols, and Bert Chase. Al and Bert had their younger brothers there. They were in the outfield, chasing fly balls.

"Hi!" Jerry greeted. "Been waiting for you!"

"Let's choose up sides," suggested Kirby. "There's enough of us here."

"Okay," said Dave.

There were ten players altogether, including Ann. She didn't seem to care that she was the only girl. Sometimes Dave's sister Mary and Bert's sister Jean would come to the field and play also, because Ann did. But they weren't here today.

Kirby and Dave were asked to be captains. They chose up sides. Dave had first choice. He picked Bobby. Ann was chosen before the two youngest boys because she was a good player, better than some of the boys. She got on Kirby's team. She seemed glad because she walked quickly to Kirby's side and smiled happily at him.

Bobby grinned. He didn't really care whose team he was on. This was for fun, anyway.

Kirby's team took last raps. Dave told his players what positions to play and in what order they were to bat. The scrub game started. The kids in the field shouted to their pitcher. "Come on, Jerry! Strike 'em out, kid! Throw 'em in there, Jerry!"

Bobby was second batter. He picked up a bat. While he waited for his turn to hit Dave came over to him.

"Did you hear that Tony might be the player picked on the All-Star team that's going to Cooperstown?" he said. "Someone told me that the men who are picking the All-Stars have been looking us over."

Bobby stared. "Tony Mandos?"

"Yep. That's what everybody's been saying. He's the best in the league, everybody says."

Bobby looked across the field at his brother Kirby. Kirby was standing with his hands on his knees near first base. He was yelling as if this was a real Grasshoppers League ball game.

"He's not better than Kirby," said Bobby seriously. "Kirby can play circles around him."

"Oh, go on, Bobby. Kirby can't hit the broad side of a barn."

Bobby flushed. "But he can field," he said. "And nobody can catch those pegs at first better than he can. And, anyway, they aren't going to choose the players yet."

Dave shrugged. "I'm just saying what I heard," he said.

Crack! The sound of bat meeting ball caught Bobby's attention. He saw the white pill fall behind second. Ann chased after it. She picked it up on a hop and pegged it to second base. The second baseman caught it easily.

"Nice throw, Ann!" Jerry yelled.

Bobby stepped to the plate. He hit the

first pitch over short, a clothesline drive to the outfield. Bobby circled the bases for a home run.

He didn't enjoy hitting that homer very much, though. After all, there were only two players in the outfield.

After a while there were three outs and Kirby's team came to bat.

Because there weren't enough players on each team, one of the rules was that a ball hit on the ground in the infield was an out.

The first two players grounded out. Kirby walked to the plate, and Bobby wished he would hit the ball. It wasn't important that Kirby was playing on the opposite team. What was important — *really* important — was for Kirby to learn to *hit the ball.*

Kirby doesn't know about an All-Star

team going to Cooperstown, thought Bobby. He doesn't know that Tony Mandos, the other first baseman for the Redbirds, will most likely go. There were a lot of guys who thought that Tony was the best first baseman in the league. Except Bobby. He'd take Kirby any day.

Kirby let a pitch go by. Then he swung hard at a pitch and missed.

"Don't try to kill it," said Jerry.

Another pitch came in. Kirby swung easier. *Crack!* The ball sailed over the right fielder's head!

Bobby almost jumped with joy. What a drive! It went for a home run. It would have been a home run even in a real game.

The next time up Kirby knocked out another long drive. The ball didn't travel as far as the first one did. But almost.

"I just swung easy!" Kirby kept saying

to Bobby and Ann after the game. "Maybe that's the secret!"

He had never been so happy in his life.

Bobby's heart swelled with pride. He told Kirby what Dave had told him, that an All-Star team was going to Cooperstown. And that everybody thought that Tony Mandos might be picked to go.

A cloud came over Kirby's face.

"Tony's good," he said. "Maybe he is the best in the league."

Bobby looked at Kirby, and then at Ann. His lips quivered.

Suddenly he cried out, "That's not true, Kirby! You're better than Tony is! Much better! You'll beat him out! Just wait and see!"

5

ON FRIDAY the Redbirds played the Seals.

The first inning went scoreless for both teams. In the second inning Dave Gessini singled through short. Mark Donahue fanned. Jerry Echols hit a long fly to left that was caught for the second out.

Kirby came to bat. He swung easy at the first pitch. Missed. He let a strike go by, then a ball. Then he swung easy again, and struck out.

Bobby watched Kirby trot, head bowed in shame, toward first base. *Don't give up, Kirby!* the cry went through Bobby's mind. *You'll beat out Tony! You will!*

The Seals got a man on in their bottom

half of the second inning. A sacrifice bunt put him on second.

Cappie became nervous again. He stepped off the mound, picked up some dirt in his hand, and dropped it. He nodded at the signal from Dave Gessini, stretched, and delivered.

"Ball one!"

"Ball two!"

At short, Bobby shook his head. Cappie never seemed to pitch very well when the pressure was on.

Cappie put over a strike, then threw two more balls, giving the batter a free ticket to first. Now there were two men on and one away.

Crack! The ball sailed over second for a double, driving in the two runners. The next Seal hitter socked a hard, bouncing grounder between short and third. It looked sure to be a hit. The runner on second made a beeline for third.

Third baseman Mark Donahue plunged after the ball. He couldn't quite reach it. Bobby raced back beyond the edge of the dirt and onto the grass. He ran as hard as he could, his eyes on the high-hopping ball. Just as the ball started to bounce past him he stuck out his gloved hand, and *caught the ball.* He stopped, and heaved the ball to first.

Bobby saw his peg going wide. Kirby would never reach that ball. Never.

But Kirby stretched his long legs, the point of his toe touching the edge of the bag. His right arm reached far out. A split second later the ball struck the pocket of his mitt and stuck there as if glued.

The crowd cheered. Horns tooted. And Bobby's heart went back where it be-

Redbirds

longed. Boy! Only Kirby could catch a wild peg like that!

That play must have helped Cappie's nerves, because he struck the next man out.

Cappie led off in the top of the third. He poled a long fly to center field. He was almost on first base before the ball came down. A sad groan broke from the throats of the Redbirds fans as the fielder made the catch.

Bobby came up and did something he had never done before. He hit four foul tips in a row to the backstop screen. He stepped away from the plate and grinned.

The people laughed and yelled at him to "Straighten one out!"

Then whiff! Bobby went down swinging!

He shook his head and smiled as he

carried the bat to the rack. Well, a guy had to strike out sometime. Even the clean-up men on major league teams struck out, didn't they?

Coach Barrows put in Bert Chase to pinch-hit for Al Dakin. Bert knocked out a single. Toby blasted a grounder to short which struck the shortstop's left foot and bounced high into the air. Bert made it safely to second, and Toby to first. The scorekeeper counted it as a hit, a ball "too hot to handle."

Bobby relaxed back in the dugout. He crossed his arms and watched Jim Hurwitz go to the plate. The Redbirds had a chance now to score a run or more. Jim was their clean-up hitter. He was big and could hit a ball farther than anybody else on the team. The Seals were leading, 2–0.

A home run would put the Redbirds ahead, 3–2. But even one run would help.

Jim swung two bats back and forth across his shoulders. He finally tossed one back to Dickie Jacobs, the mascot, then stepped into the batter's box.

Sam Wood, the red-headed southpaw for the Seals, was very careful with his pitches to Jim. He must have tried hard to cut the corners with his first three pitches. But he missed each time for a count of three balls. Then he threw one down the middle, and Jim swung.

Crack! The ball sailed out to left field. It curved over the fielder's head, struck the fence and bounced back. The fielder picked it up and pegged it in.

Both runners scored, and Jim stopped on third for a triple. With the score tied,

Dave Gessini came up. He hit a hot grounder down the third-base line which went foul by inches. Then Wood threw three balls in succession, making the count three and one.

"Wait 'em out!" yelled Coach Barrows. He paced back and forth.

Dave let the next pitch go by.

"Strike two!"

"Okay! If it's in there, hit it!"

Wood took his time with the next pitch. This was the one that counted. If it was outside the strike zone, Dave would walk. If it was over, Dave might whack it and knock in another run.

Crack! The ball bounced hard across the infield to short. The shortstop moved in, caught the hop, and pegged to first.

Out!

"Close," said Coach Barrows. "But not

close enough. Okay, fellas. Get out there and get 'em out!"

The Seals put a man on in the bottom half of the third, but he failed to score.

Don Robinson, pinch-hitting for Mark, led off for the Redbirds. He singled with a sharp drive through the pitcher's box. Jerry Echols followed with a Texas leaguer between short and third. The third-base coach held Don up at second.

Kirby came to bat. Bobby watched from the dugout. Here was Kirby's chance again to knock in runs.

"Come on, Kirby!" a high-pitched voice shouted from the stands. "Hit it, Kirby!"

Bobby grinned. That was Ann. She was rooting for Kirby, too.

Kirby swung at the first pitch. There was a solid crack as bat met ball. The ball rose high into the air toward left field.

Kirby dropped his bat and ran hard for first. Bobby leaped out of the dugout, his heart singing.

I bet that's a homer! I bet that's a homer!

Then the ball struck the grass just outside of the white foul line. Bobby groaned.

"Foul ball!" yelled the umpire.

The runners returned to their bases. Kirby ran back to the plate and picked up his bat. His lower lip was tugged over his upper one. What tough luck, thought Bobby. Kirby just could never get a break.

Kirby took a called strike, then a ball. Then he swung hard at a low pitch and struck out. Bobby shook his head sadly.

Cappie blasted a hard grounder through second, scoring a run to break the tie. Bobby and Bert went down to end the inning.

Tony Mandos took Kirby's place at first base. He caught a couple of wide throws, one from Bobby, the other from Don Robinson. Bobby thought that if Tony hadn't such a big web on his mitt he would never have caught those throws. Kirby would have made those catches look easy.

Neither team scored in the fifth. In the last inning Tony came to bat with Don on first and one out. He punched out a solid line drive over the shortstop's head. Bobby had to admit that that was a good, clean hit. No doubt that Tony was a better hitter than Kirby. But without that special mitt of his, Tony could not compare with Kirby as a first baseman. Kirby was left-handed and Tony was right-handed. That, itself, was in Kirby's favor. Also, Kirby was at least an inch taller. He could reach out farther to catch wide throws.

That mitt, thought Bobby. It was only that mitt that would make the officials choose Tony over Kirby.

Nobody knocked Don and Tony in.

The Seals came up for their last time at bat. They belted out a single. The next hitter walloped a sizzling grounder to Bobby. He fielded it, tossed the ball to second. Second to first. Double play!

The next hitter flied out and the game was over. The Redbirds won, 3–2.

6

AT HOME Kirby wanted Bobby to throw to him while he batted.

"Pitch to me, will you, Bobby?" he pleaded. "I need batting practice. That's why I can't hit."

Bobby did not feel like pitching. He said, "Who's going to chase 'em?"

"Ann. She'll chase 'em. Won't you, Ann?"

"Yes. I'll chase 'em."

Bobby looked at them both disgustedly. He wanted to go swimming. The day was hot and he hadn't gone swimming since sometime last week.

"Why not go swimming instead?" he

said. "We just got through playing baseball."

"We can go swimming tomorrow," said Kirby. "Come on. Will you, Bobby? Please?"

Bobby pressed his lips together and crossed his arms. Baseball. Baseball. That's all Kirby ever thought about.

"You like swimming. You like looking for spiders and toads and ants, don't you?" Ann said to him. Her voice was hard.

Bobby looked at her. Her eyes were hard, too. "Sure, I do," he said. "Why? Just because you and Kirby don't like to do that doesn't mean nobody should."

"That's not what I mean," replied Ann. "You can look for those insects without anybody helping you. With baseball it's different. Nobody can play baseball by himself, can he?"

Bobby realized what she meant. "Of course not. But we've played a lot of baseball today, already. Can't we wait till tomorrow?"

Ann's eyes snapped. "In the first place, I see that you don't care whether Kirby gets picked on the All-Star team or not. Maybe you want Tony Mandos picked. In the second place, you need a lot of practice yourself, throwing. All right. Go swimming if Mom will let you, and I bet she won't. I'll play with Kirby myself. I can pitch."

Ann clutched Kirby's arm and began to pull him toward the field where the kids played baseball. Bobby stared after them. He could not let Ann and Kirby be mad at him. Maybe he would want them to do something with him sometime.

He uncrossed his arms and ran after

them. "Ann! Kirby! Wait! I've changed my mind!"

Ann and Kirby stopped.

"Wait for me! I'll get my glove!" said Bobby.

Ann played the outfield. Bobby pitched. They played for ten or fifteen minutes. Out of all the pitches Bobby threw Kirby hit only two flies to the outfield. Most of the pitches he either fouled to the backstop screen or missed entirely.

Bobby didn't say anything. Kirby just could not hit that ball. When Bobby threw slower, Kirby told him to throw harder.

Presently, Ann shouted from the outfield, "Wait a minute, Bobby! Don't pitch!"

Bobby looked over his shoulder. What did she want to do? Bat, too?

Ann ran in, her pony tail flopping. She went up to Kirby.

"Kirby, may I tell you something? I mean about hitting?"

Kirby stared at her. So did Bobby.

"What are you going to tell me?" said Kirby, his voice hurt. "That I can't hit? I know I can't. That's why I want to practice."

"No," said Ann. "But I borrowed a book from the library. I've read the whole book already. It tells how to play all the positions on the diamond. And it tells how to bat."

Kirby looked at her puzzledly. "*You* borrowed the book on baseball? Why didn't you tell me about it? Is it good?"

"It's very good," said Ann. "There's a chapter about hitting. One of the major league ballplayers wrote it. He says that a lot of hitters hold their hands about two inches from the end of the bat. They hit much better that way."

"I know what that is," Bobby broke in. "That's choking up on the bat."

"That's right," said Ann. "Why don't you try that, Kirby? Choke up on the bat. Maybe you'll hit better."

Kirby shrugged. "You can't get distance that way."

"But hits are better than getting distance once in a blue moon, aren't they?" said Ann. Her voice was sharp, drawing the attention of both boys quickly. "You can't get on base if you don't get hits, can you? And how do you expect to be picked on the All-Star team —"

She stopped. Her lips trembled, and for a moment Bobby thought she was going

to cry. She really wanted Kirby to learn how to hit. You seldom saw a sister *that* interested in her brother. Imagine, thought Bobby. And she had gone so far as to borrow a book on baseball, just to help out Kirby!

"All right," said Kirby. "I'll try it. I've tried everything else, I guess."

"Okay," Ann said. Her eyes brightened. "Wait till I get back out there."

Bobby walked to the mound with the ball. He waited till Ann was in the outfield, then pitched to Kirby. He threw the first pitch as hard as he could. Kirby fouled it. Then Kirby began to hit some of the pitches solidly. He smiled as pitch after pitch sailed to the outfield.

Finally Ann yelled from the outfield, "I'm tired of running! Let's quit!"

Bobby was tired, too, but he wasn't

going to stop until either Ann or Kirby said so. He wanted Kirby to be picked on the All-Star team as much as Ann did.

On Thursday, the Redbirds tackled the Mustangs. The game was tied 6–6 and had to go into an extra inning. With a man on first and two away, a Mustang hitter banged out a triple to score the winning run.

In that game, Kirby was up twice and hit a single. In the following games against the Gulls and the Panthers he did well, too. He hit the ball both times up in the game with the Gulls. Both times the ball was caught and Kirby was thrown out. But the important thing was — he was hitting. In the Panther game he struck out once, and singled.

But Tony Mandos was playing excellent ball, too. Already he had hit two home runs, a triple, and two doubles since the season had started. Bobby thought that some of the throws that Tony had missed on first base Kirby would have caught. But Tony was doing a fine job. Everybody was saying that Tony Mandos was certain to be picked on the All-Star team.

It's his glove, Bobby told himself. Without that web on his mitt, Tony would not have a chance against Kirby.

Kirby was hitting better. That was definite. He did not hit the ball very far, but he was getting on base more often than he used to. Choking up on the bat had helped him a lot. Thanks to Ann.

But Kirby was a whiz on first. Everybody could see that. He was getting men out in very close plays, plays which otherwise might have meant runs for the opposing teams. Every time Kirby made a long stretch to catch a wild peg, the people cheered and applauded. They wouldn't do that if he wasn't good, would they?

On Friday afternoon, a hot and sticky day, Bobby, Kirby, and Ann put on their bathing suits and went swimming down by the bridge. They passed Tony's house. A blue car trimmed with shining chrome stood in the driveway. It was Mr. Mandos's car.

"Let's see if Tony wants to come with us," suggested Kirby.

He went to the house while Ann and Bobby waited.

Soon he came back out. "Tony's already at the pond," he said.

There were a lot of other kids swimming in the pond, too. Tony saw them and swam over. "Hi!" he said. "I wondered if you were coming! The water's great!"

Bobby didn't swim around with Tony. He didn't want to get too friendly with him. Tony was on their baseball team; that was friendship enough.

Bobby climbed up the bank, walked along the edge of the bridge, and dived into the water. He got more fun out of diving than swimming. He wished that the bridge was higher. Boy! Would that be fun, then!

After a while the kids began to leave. Tony left, too. At last Bobby, Kirby, and Ann left. Just as they reached their house a blue car zipped past. It was the Mandoses'.

Bobby stared after it a minute. "Was Tony in it?" he asked.

"I think so," said Kirby. "But I'm not sure. Why?"

Bobby shrugged. "Oh — nothing."

They went into the house and dressed. Then Bobby told his mother he was going bike riding for a while.

He rode slowly down the road. He didn't want to pump fast. Somebody watching might get curious. Terry followed him, yipping at the rear wheel.

At last Bobby reached Tony Mandos's house. He parked the bike in the driveway. He walked around the house quietly. Terry trailed after him, his nose close to the grass. He sniffed as if he were on the track of something.

Since Tony wasn't home, Bobby had a chance to look for Tony's first-base mitt. Bobby didn't know what he would do with it if he found it. But he would do *something.*

He looked hard around the yard. Finally he saw it on the front porch. His heart pounded. It was the mitt all right — the mitt with the big web. The mitt which Tony used to make those great catches.

Bobby went on the porch, picked up the mitt.

Just then Tony Mandos came out of the door.

"Hello, Bobby. What are you doing here?" he asked.

7

BOBBY stared. His face grew hot. He could hardly answer Tony. He had been sure that Tony was in his father's car.

"Hi – hi, Tony," he managed to say finally. "I just rode down to see if you were here."

Tony smiled. His crow-black hair was combed neatly back. He was wearing blue jeans and a blue and white striped T-shirt. He came off the porch and looked at the mitt in Bobby's hand.

"How do you like that mitt?" he asked proudly.

Bobby swallowed. He forced a grin to

his lips. "It's a beauty. I don't think anybody's could beat it."

"I don't, either," said Tony. "Except your brother Kirby's."

Bobby frowned. "Kirby's? This is better than Kirby's. Don't you think so?"

Tony shrugged. He took the mitt from Bobby and slipped his left hand into it. He tugged at the leather-laced web.

"Kirby's doesn't have a web like mine," he said. "With a web like this almost anybody could catch a ball."

"What's wrong with that? It's legal, isn't it?" All of a sudden Bobby didn't know what to think of Tony. Before this he had never talked much with Tony Mandos.

"Sure, it's legal," replied Tony. He shrugged again. "I don't know. I guess it's all right." He turned and looked at Terry sniffing around the yard. "That your dog?"

Bobby nodded. "Yes. His name's Terry. He's a Scotty."

"We heard on the radio that a mad dog was loose somewhere around town," said Tony. He grinned. "Guess it wasn't yours, was it?"

Bobby laughed. "Not Terry! How long ago did you hear that, Tony?"

"About an hour ago."

"What kind of a dog was it?"

"I don't know. I didn't pay much attention. Mom and Dad heard it, and they spoke about it. Guess by now it's caught, anyway."

"Oh, sure," said Bobby.

Bobby was thinking more about what he had come here for than about the mad dog. He felt guilty and ashamed. Tony was a lot different than he had imagined.

Even though Bobby played baseball with him, he hadn't known Tony very well. Now, just in these few moments of talking with Tony, Bobby had learned a lot about what kind of a guy he was.

Suddenly, Bobby was glad that Tony was home. It would have been terrible to have taken a mitt from a guy like Tony. Guess maybe it would have been terrible to take the mitt anyway, Bobby thought. The feeling of guilt grew worse, as if it were something that had come alive inside him. He hoped that Tony would not notice how he acted.

Maybe if they did something together —

"Want to go for a hike?" Bobby suggested. His breath came fast. He couldn't ever let Tony know what he had really come here for.

Tony looked up. He grinned. “Down through the gully?”

Bobby’s face brightened. “Sure!”

“Okay!”

Tony tossed the mitt onto the porch. He ran toward the bridge where the kids swam. Bobby followed close behind. Once he looked back to see if Terry was following. But Terry had found something in the yard and was playing with it. He was growling and rolling over and over with whatever it was. It looked like an old shoe. That Terry could have fun with anything, thought Bobby, feeling much better.

Bobby walked behind Tony down along the creek. They walked carefully over the large, flat rocks. Some of the rocks were slimy and slippery. In different places trees had fallen over the creek.

The boys climbed onto the fallen trees and walked the full length to the other side. Then they climbed off and walked again along the wet rocks.

The creek water was wide in some places, narrow in others; deep in some places, shallow in others.

"Look!" said Tony suddenly.

Bobby almost collided with Tony as he brought himself to a quick stop. He looked at where Tony pointed. A thin black snake was swimming in one of the shallow places. The water was so clear that the snake's whole weaving body — about twenty inches of it — was easily seen.

They saw crabs, too, crawling in the crystal-clear bottom. And polliwogs. And minnows. And skippers on top of the water.

"Boy!" gasped Bobby. "Would I like to camp around here sometime!"

"Me, too," said Tony.

Bobby told Tony about the tent he and Kirby had in the small woods above their house. And about the deer that had been feeding on their vegetables.

"Wow!" said Tony. "That must've been fun!"

"It was," said Bobby.

Now the rocky sides of the creek were higher. The trees that grew on the banks on either side towered high above their heads. Thin slices of golden sunlight shimmered at their feet.

Just beyond them was a waterfall. It was five or six feet high. Not much water flowed over it now, though.

"Watch yourself," cautioned Tony.

The boys climbed down the dry, sharp-edged rocks alongside the waterfall. They reached the bottom. The water gave off a hollow sound as it spilled down. It foamed up at the bottom like a big pot of boiling water.

"Bobby!" Tony whispered. "Look! A dog!"

Bobby whirled. A brown, curly-coated dog was standing on a rock directly in front of them. His beady eyes were fastened on the boys. A low growl broke from his throat.

"Where did he come from?" asked Bobby.

"He just got here," said Tony. "He's breathing hard. He must have been running."

"Wonder whose dog he is?"

"I don't know. Maybe his owner's name is on his tag. I'll take a look."

He started forward.

The dog held his ground. He growled again. His eyes flashed angrily. His lips curled back.

"Wait, Tony!" said Bobby. He was staring at the dog's mouth. "Tony, you don't think that he's the mad dog your folks heard about on the radio, do you?"

Tony stared. "I – I don't know!"

"Look at his mouth!"

Froth was at the corners of the dog's open jaws.

"He doesn't look good to me," said Tony huskily. "But how do you know he's mad? Ever see a mad dog before?"

"No. I – I just *feel* it!"

"Me, too."

Bobby's heart hammered. He didn't dare move. He knew that Tony was trembling beside him, too.

"I think we're in his way," said Tony. "He wants to get above the waterfall."

The dog took a step toward them. His lips curled up a little more. Another growl broke from his throat.

The boys stepped back. But they were definitely in the dog's way. They could not go either side. The water prevented them on their left. The high, rocky wall stopped them on their right.

Bobby felt sweat stream down his face. "What are we going to do, Tony?"

8

TONY didn't answer immediately. He was listening to something. A moment later he said, "Bobby! Somebody's coming!"

A man came into view around a bend a short way down the creek. Other men were behind him. Two of them held large nets at the end of poles. A third man held a shotgun.

"Now I'm sure it's the mad dog!" cried Bobby. "Those men are looking for him!"

The dog's head lowered. He took another step forward.

Bobby backed up against Tony. "I think he's going to charge, Tony!"

They backed against the wall.

The men saw them. They saw the dog, too, and started forward slightly faster.

"Don't move, boys," one of the men said. "That dog is mad."

As if we didn't know, thought Bobby.

But what could the men do? That dog had run away from them before. It would run again. The man with the shotgun would not dare shoot. Not with Bobby and Tony in front of him.

Bobby held his breath. There wasn't much space between them and the water. The dog could run past them easily enough. But maybe it wouldn't. Maybe, being mad, it would attack them. Bobby shivered as he thought about it.

The men were walking slower, now. They advanced closer and closer. They wore high-topped shoes which were good for walking on rocks like these.

Suddenly, the dog's ears perked up. He looked behind him.

Bobby's heart skipped a beat. What would the dog do now?

Quickly, the dog turned his head back toward the boys.

"Here, Rex!" said the nearest man softly. "Here, Rex! Come here, boy!"

Just then Tony moved from Bobby's side – and stood directly in the path of the dog!

"Tony!" Bobby shrilled. "Get back here!"

"Sh!" said Tony. He remained still, looking straight at the dog. His lips were pressed into a thin line. You could tell he was scared, but he stood there just the same.

He's crazy! thought Bobby. He shouldn't do that!

"Here, Rex, boy," the man said again. He was three or four feet away from the dog, now. "Come here, boy."

The dog looked around again. Then he looked at Tony. He seemed confused. He stopped growling.

"Here, Rex. Easy, boy. Just take it easy, now."

The man took another step forward. He whipped the net over the dog's head. The dog yipped in anger. He fell back on his rear legs and tried hard to free himself. The other man dropped his net and rushed forward. He grabbed hold of the dog's collar. The dog kicked hard, but the grip on his collar was too much for him. The net was taken off and a muzzle put over his face.

Bobby took a deep breath and let it out. Boy! What a close call *that* was!

The men looked at the boys and grinned. The man who held the dog said, "Thanks, boys, for helping us catch my dog. Rex got bit by a rabid fox while I was out hunting with him. I got the fox all right, but Rex got rabies from the bite."

Bobby shook his head. "Boy! He sure gave us a scare!"

The man chuckled. "He gave us a scare, too. A mad dog might do anything, you know." Then he looked at Tony with pride. "You were mighty brave to get in the path of Rex like that, kid. You were taking a chance doing that."

"I guess I was," said Tony quietly. "But if he came after me, I was ready to jump aside."

Bobby grinned at him. Nobody would have done what Tony had done. That took a lot of nerve. Except, maybe, Kirby. Kirby had a lot of nerve, too.

"What are your names, boys?" the man asked.

"I'm Tony Mandos and this is Bobby Jamison," said Tony.

The man opened his mouth in surprise. "Well, what do you know? I know your dads."

"You do?" Bobby's brows shot up.

"Sure do. I'm Ben Watkins. Tell them I said hello. So long, boys. We have to be going. And thanks again for your help."

The men walked down the creek, then climbed the bank to the road.

Bobby sighed with relief. He felt tired from the excitement of coming face to face with the mad dog. "Want to go back, Tony? I think I'd better get home."

"Okay."

They returned to Tony's house. Terry dashed around a corner, his ears perked up and his short tail whipping back and forth. He nipped playfully at Bobby's pant legs.

"Hey, cut that out!" said Bobby. "Come on. We're going home."

"Wait a minute," interrupted Tony. "My mitt's gone."

Bobby stared. "Isn't it on the porch?"

Tony searched the porch carefully. "I don't see it."

Bobby turned a suspicious look at Terry. Terry stood with his front legs spread apart, his tongue hanging out one side of his mouth and his tail snapping back and forth like a short whip. If Terry was guilty of taking the glove, he certainly did not show it. But, who except Terry could have taken it?

Bobby helped Tony look for the mitt. They searched around the house and all around the yard. They could not find it.

A car turned into the driveway. Tony's parents were home.

Bobby's heart ached. Only a little while ago he had wanted to take Tony's glove and hide it somewhere so that Tony could not use it in a ball game. Now, he wanted to find it more than anything. He had learned to like Tony a lot in the last hour or so. Tony was very different than Bobby had expected him to be. He was better than just all right. He was — well, he was pretty wonderful.

"I'm sorry, Tony," Bobby said seriously. "If you can't find it, I'll be back tomorrow and help you look for it."

Tony pressed his lips tightly together.

He said, "We play the Mustangs tomorrow. If I don't find my glove, I'll have to borrow one from somebody."

Bobby thought a moment. "If you were only a lefty, then you could use Kirby's. I'll help you borrow one, Tony, but first let's look some more tomorrow."

Bobby scolded Terry on the way home. Terry must have understood; his ears drooped, and he wagged his tail very slowly.

Bobby told Kirby and Ann about the mad dog. Then he told them about Tony's missing mitt. They searched for it the next morning. They covered the ground thoroughly around Tony's house. But, no mitt.

It was almost noon when the three of them – Kirby, Ann, and Bobby – returned home. Bobby was very sad. He felt as though he was responsible for Tony's missing mitt.

Kirby started at first base for the Redbirds that afternoon in the game against the Mustangs. He got on base once on an error. In the bottom of the third inning, Tony took Kirby's place. The first baseman for the Mustangs let Tony use his glove.

Bobby hoped that no grounders would come down to him at short. He'd been thinking about Tony's missing mitt. But with men on second and third a high, bouncing ball was hit down between short and third. Bobby ran to his right. He caught the ball. He took it in his bare hand and very carefully tried to throw a perfect peg to Tony.

He heaved it. The ball sailed high —

and wide. Tony jumped off the base after it. He still could not reach it. The ball hit the grass behind first and the runner went to second. The men on second and third scored.

The next man flied out to end the inning. The score was 6–3, with the Redbirds on the short end.

Bobby sat way at the end of the bench in the dugout. He felt pretty awful about that peg. Kirby came and sat down beside him. He looked strangely at Bobby.

"You didn't throw that ball wild on purpose, did you, Bobby?" he asked quietly.

Bobby stared at him as if he had been hit with a rock. Then he looked at some of the others who were watching him. He saw by their faces that they were thinking the same thing!

"Of course not, Kirby!" he whispered huskily. "I — I could *never* do a thing like that!"

Coach Barrows stopped in front of Bobby and said, "I think you probably tighten up out there, Bobby. Loosen up! And don't hurry your throw, unless you have to."

9

BOBBY wished that Coach Barrows would take him out of the game and put someone else in. After what Kirby had said to him, and the way the other boys looked at him, he did not feel like playing any more. How could they ever think he would throw a wild peg to Tony Mandos on purpose? That was *crazy!*

He remembered that only yesterday he had wanted to take Tony's glove and hide it. Thinking of that made him feel ashamed again. But he knew that if he had taken the mitt, he would not have kept it hidden very long. He would have returned it to Tony.

Dave Gessini, Mike Bliss, and Tony

were up at bat in that order. Mike Bliss was a utility outfielder. He was a tall redhead with glasses. He was taking Jerry Echols's place.

Dave pounded out a screaming single through second base. Then Mike got up and fouled the first two pitches. He tapped his bat against the plate a lot, and almost did not raise it in time for the third pitch.

"Ball!" said the umpire.

"He was lucky then," said Kirby. He raised his voice and yelled at Mike, "Keep your bat up, Mike! Be ready!"

A chest-high pitch came in. Mike swung. *Crack!* The ball sizzled along the grass toward short. The Mustangs shortstop reached down. The ball struck the thumb of his glove and glanced away from him. He raced after it, but there would be no play.

Dave crossed second. He went past it a few steps, then returned to the bag and stood on it with both feet. Mike held up on first.

"Now's our chance," Kirby said. "Who's up? Oh – Tony."

Bobby saw him bite on his lower lip. He wondered what Kirby could be thinking. Was he hoping that Tony wouldn't get a hit?

"Come on, Tony!" Kirby suddenly shouted. "Drive that apple out of the lot!"

Bobby didn't know how to feel about Tony's getting a hit. A hit would score a run or two, depending on how far the ball traveled. A hit would also help Tony have a better chance of being selected on the All-Star team. Yet, no matter how much Bobby liked Tony, he still wanted Kirby to be selected.

Crack! A long fly toward left field! The ball was going – going. It was GONE! It had sailed over the fence for a home run!

Horns blared. The Redbirds fans whistled and cheered. Tony's long, powerful clout had tied the score.

Everybody in the dugout climbed out and shook Tony's hand. Bobby felt funny inside. He didn't know whether he was happy that Tony had knocked the homer or not. Sure, the score was tied now, 6–6. But Tony probably had made good his chances of being chosen on the All-Star team.

Cappie fouled out to the first baseman. Bobby, with two and two on him, lined a Texas leaguer to short. The shortstop speared it for the second out. Al Dakin wiggled at the plate, then blasted a beautiful double between left and center fields. He died on second when Toby Warren swung at a high pitch for his third strike, missing the ball by a foot.

The Mustangs pushed over a run in the bottom of the fourth to lead again. The Redbirds came to raps, eager to put on another rally. But the Mustangs held them.

In the sixth the Redbirds got a man as far as third. The Mustangs played great defensive ball, and held him there till the third out was called.

The Redbirds lost, 7–6.

"That's all right, fellas," said Mr. Barrows. "That was a great game. Nice sock, Tony. You really blasted that ball hard."

Tony grinned shyly. "Thanks, Coach," he said.

On the way home in Mr. Jamison's car, Bobby said to Tony, "I'm sorry about that bad throw, Tony. I didn't mean it."

"I know you didn't," said Tony. "Forget it."

"But everybody thought I did it on purpose," said Bobby.

"On purpose?" Tony's brows arched. "Why should you do it on purpose?"

Bobby met Tony's eyes. He knew that Tony was sincere. He knew that, at least, Tony had never thought that Bobby had thrown the ball wild on purpose.

"That's what I'd like to know," answered Bobby.

But all the other boys thought he had a reason, he told himself. They believed he had done it to make Tony look poor on first base.

"I wish I could find my mitt, though,"

said Tony worriedly. "I'm more used to it. It's expensive, too. Dad paid about fifty dollars for it."

"We'll look for it after supper," promised Kirby. "We'll all come down and help again."

Bobby looked at his tall, dark-haired brother. His face flashed a big, pleased smile.

After supper Bobby, Kirby, and Ann walked to Tony's house. Terry went with them. He ran ahead of them all the way, his short tail snapping back and forth like a toy that was wound up too tight.

Tony came out of the house and they all started to look for his mitt.

"I bet it's gone for good," said Tony hopelessly. "I'll never find it."

"It's Terry's fault," said Bobby. "He's the one that carried it away."

"Don't blame Terry," said Ann, in defense of the dog all three of them loved so dearly. "You brought him along with you."

Bobby's eyes lowered. Yes, that was true. It was his fault more than anyone else's that Tony's glove was missing.

Perhaps he should buy a new mitt for Tony. He could start selling magazines, or cut lawns to raise the money. Yes, that's what he could do.

They searched underneath the porch, around Mrs. Mandos's hollyhocks and rose-bushes, and in the garden. It was almost dark.

Suddenly Ann shouted, "Look! Look what Terry's got!"

All the boys looked. There was Terry, trotting proudly from the direction of the road. And dangling from his mouth was Tony's mitt!

"He must have had it hidden inside the culvert!" cried Tony happily. "Who'd ever think to look for it there!"

Kirby grinned as he took the mitt from Terry's mouth. "All right, Terry. Nice work. But why didn't you find it before?"

Ann's face was bright with joy and relief. "I guess he just wanted us to sweat it out for a while."

Bobby fell on his knees. He clutched the little terrier into his arms. He rubbed his face against the dog's warm body. "You little mutt," he said. "It's a good thing you found that glove! You saved me a lot of hard work and money!"

10

DURING the next few days, before their upcoming game with the Seals, Bobby, Kirby, and some of the other members of the team practiced on the pasture field. Tony practiced with them. Bobby played his regular position at shortstop. Tony played first base when Kirby was batting.

Bobby, as usual, caught most of the grounders hit to him. Most of his pegs to first were pretty good. But on his wide or high throws, Tony often failed to catch them. Even his big-webbed mitt was not enough for him to snare those throws. His legs and arms just were not long enough.

The throws had to be fairly close to him for him to make the catches.

But at the plate Tony was a slugger. Every time he batted he pounded the old apple a tremendous distance into the outfield.

Kirby was practically the opposite. He was tall. His arms and legs were rangy. He could stretch far out and catch nearly all of Bobby's wild pegs. But at the plate Kirby just could not swing the bat on the same line the ball came in on. He either swung over it or under it. Sometimes he met the ball squarely. When he did his face lit up like a Christmas candle. But the next time up he would strike out.

When the boys practiced on the pasture field again, Bobby didn't go. He said he wanted to find some praying mantises to add to his collection. That wasn't the real reason, though. He didn't want to go because it hurt him to see Kirby swing at so many pitches at the plate and miss.

Bobby could hardly understand that. He had tried a long time to figure out why Kirby was such a poor hitter. Even choking up on the bat did not help him very much. It seems so easy to me, Bobby thought. I swing at the ball where I see it, and I hit it almost every time. Why can't Kirby do that?

The sky was gray with scattered clouds on the day the Redbirds tangled with the Seals. Bobby pulled on his jersey and cap and got his glove from the clothes closet.

"What are you waiting for, Kirby?" he said. His brother was sitting in the living room, reading a book. "Mr. Gessini will be coming after us any minute."

"I'm not going," said Kirby, without glancing up from the book.

Bobby's mouth fell open. "You're not *going?*" His voice was almost a shrill cry. "Why not?"

"I quit," said Kirby.

"You *can't* quit!"

Kirby burst out of the chair with his book. He stomped heavily across the floor to his room. "Who said I can't?" he said loudly, and slammed the door behind him.

Bobby's mother entered the living room from the kitchen. She had a pen in her hand. She had been writing a letter to someone – maybe answering the letter she had received yesterday from her mother in Maryland.

She looked toward Kirby's door, then turned wide, puzzled eyes at Bobby. "Did he say he has quit playing baseball?" she asked.

Bobby nodded. "That's what he said."

"Why did he quit?"

Bobby shrugged. "I don't know, Mom. Maybe he thinks he hasn't been playing well."

His mother took her pen back into the kitchen. Then she went to Kirby's room. Bobby heard her say something to Kirby, and heard Kirby answer. But their voices were so soft and muffled he could not make out what they said.

After a while Mrs. Jamison came out of the room.

"Isn't he coming, Mom?" Bobby asked.

She shook her head. "No. He doesn't want to. And nothing I say helps. You go alone, Bobby."

"What shall I tell Mr. Barrows?"

Mrs. Jamison thought a moment. She shrugged her shoulders. "Just tell him Kirby doesn't want to play."

Two deep furrows appeared between Bobby's eyebrows as he walked to the door. He knew how Kirby felt, all right. He knew exactly.

Bobby waited on the porch. Soon Mr. Gessini came along with his car. Bobby got in.

"Where's Kirby?" Jim Hurwitz asked. Jim was sitting in the front seat with Dave and Mr. Gessini.

"He doesn't want to come," replied Bobby.

Jim and Dave looked at him strangely. "Why not?" said Dave.

Bobby climbed into the back seat. "I don't know," he said.

They stopped for Tony Mandos. Tony

also asked where Kirby was. Bobby told him.

"Maybe he doesn't feel well," said Tony.

Nobody said anything.

Coach Barrows also wondered why Kirby didn't show up. Bobby told him the same thing he had told the others.

"Well, looks as if Tony will play the whole game," said Mr. Barrows simply. "But it's up to you, Bobby, to make those throws good to first base. Take your time. Tony can't stretch out as far as Kirby can, you know."

"I'll try," promised Bobby.

The Seals had first raps. For the Redbirds Curt Barrows had the line-up arranged as follows:

B. JAMISON — shortstop
A. DAKIN — second base
T. WARREN — left field

J. Hurwitz — center field
D. Gessini — catcher
M. Donahue — third base
J. Echols — right field
T. Mandos — first base
J. Nichols — pitcher

The umpire named off the batteries for both teams. Then the Redbirds ran out to the field amid a roar of applause and horn-blowing.

The Seals lead-off man took a called strike, then hit a dribbling grounder to third. Mark fielded it and threw him out with a perfect peg to first.

I wish I could throw that straight, thought Bobby.

The second hitter popped to first. The next hitter went the full count, then walked.

The clean-up man looked over the first

two pitches — one a ball, the other a strike. He belted the next just out of reach of pitcher Jack Nichols's outstretched glove. Second baseman Al Dakin ran and made a stab at the ball. He caught it, tossed it underhand to Bobby, who raced hard to cover second. Out!

Bobby, leading off in the last of the first, clouted the second pitch for a single. He got the steal signal from Mr. Barrows. As the ball zipped past the plate, Bobby took off like a jet. He slid safely into second, beating the throw by two feet.

Bobby was in scoring position now. All that was needed was a hit.

Dakin fanned. Toby hit a two-three pitch solidly to left field, but it was caught. Two outs. Bobby crossed his arms and stiffened his lips. Couldn't anybody knock him in?

Jim Hurwitz came up. *Crack!* A Texas leaguer over short. Bobby shot to third, touched the corner of the bag with his toe, and bolted hard for home. He scored standing up. Dave Gessini then flied out to center, ending the inning.

The next two innings went by scoreless for both teams.

In the top of the fourth, the Seals lead-off man banged a hot grounder to Bobby's right side. Bobby fielded it nicely, pegged to first. A sick cry broke from his lips. The ball was wide! Tony Mandos couldn't reach it, and the hitter was on.

Bobby shook his head. Kirby would have caught that.

The bad throw started off a rally for the Seals. They scored five runs. Mr. Barrows took Jack out and put in Cappie Brennan. The rally stopped.

The Redbirds went hitless at their turn at bat. And Bobby took all the blame himself. That bad peg had started it all.

In the fifth Tony missed another wide throw. This time the ball was thrown by second baseman Don Robinson, who had taken Al Dakin's place. Cappie Brennan then threw in a home run pitch, which raised the Seals' score to 7. The Redbirds managed to put three runs across when they batted, but it was not enough.

In the sixth inning neither team hit safely. The game ended with the Seals winning, 7–4.

"You have to come to the next game!" Bobby pleaded with Kirby that night. "We would've won today if you had played first. I made three bad throws. One of them started the rally. I know you would've caught those throws, Kirby. Everybody else said so, too."

"Well, your throws should have been better," said Kirby quietly. "And I've played before, and we still lost."

"That's not so," said Bobby. "You helped us win two or three games by your catches at first. But that's not the only reason you should go to the next game. Mr. Barrows said that scouts will be there."

"Scouts?" Kirby frowned.

"You know! The men who are choosing the All-Stars," said Bobby. "They're going to be there to make the final selections for the All-Star game in Cooperstown. You *can't* miss that, Kirby."

Kirby's face dropped. "But I will. I'm not going. Tony's better than I am, anyway. They'll pick him, whether I'm there or not."

A lump that felt like a golf ball rose in Bobby's throat. It hurt him to see Kirby feeling like this. "You *must* go, Kirby," he insisted. "You're better than Tony. I know you are. They'll pick you for sure."

"I said I'm not going and that's final!" Kirby almost shouted.

Bobby stepped back from the whip-cracking sound of Kirby's voice. He walked out of the room, Kirby's harsh words ringing in his ears.

On Friday, Bobby rode to the game again with Mr. Gessini, Dave, Jim, and Tony. His own father had not come home from work yet.

Bobby felt very bad. For the first time in his life he was ashamed of his brother Kirby. He had always thought that Kirby had plenty of nerve to face any kind of situation.

"I wish Kirby had come," Tony said. "Now those men won't be able to see him play again. They've seen him before and they might pick him if he was here."

Bobby looked up at Tony. Tears stung his eyes.

"That's exactly what I told Kirby," he said. "But he wouldn't listen. No matter what I said, he wouldn't listen to me."

11

SOME of the Mustangs players were at the field already. Bobby recognized Earl Lowe warming up. Earl was a tall, slender boy whose fire-red hair stuck out from under his black baseball cap like dried-up straw. He was a southpaw, one of the best pitchers in the league.

"Oh-oh," Dave murmured. "You see who's starting for the Mustangs today?"

"Lowe?" Jim pushed out his lower lip. "Aw, he's not so hot. A couple of hits and he'll go to pieces."

"I hope," said Tony, and laughed.

Curt Barrows and six or seven Redbirds were playing pitch and catch.

"Where's Kirby?" asked Mr. Barrows.

"He's not coming," said Bobby.

"Why not? Doesn't he want to play baseball any more?" Mr. Barrows sounded very serious.

Bobby's heart thumped nervously. "I guess not."

The coach shook his head disgustedly. "Did he know that a couple of men were going to be here today to look over the players?"

Bobby nodded. "I think so."

"Is that why he didn't want to come?"

Bobby's heart beat harder. "I don't know."

Stop asking me questions about Kirby! he wanted to shout. I wanted him to come to the game. He didn't want to. He's home. He's sitting in the living room, reading or watching TV. I know what you're thinking. You're thinking that he's afraid to come because it will hurt him if he isn't picked on the All-Star team. Well – it's true. I know that, too. And say it if you want to. Say he hasn't got what it takes! Because I know that is true, too!

Kirby *can* play ball, though. He can play first base better than any other player in the league. He doesn't always hit, but he isn't the poorest hitter, either! He's better than Tony Mandos, or any other first baseman you care to name. He's the best in the league! I know those men would pick him if he played today. But *he* doesn't. He doesn't think he's any good at all.

Ask *him* why he didn't come! Don't ask me!

Bobby swallowed hard. He picked up

a ball and called to Dave Gessini. "Come on, Dave. Let's play catch."

After a while the Mustangs had their infield warm-up. When they were finished, the Redbirds had theirs.

Bobby wished that black clouds would come sweeping across the blue sky and pour rain down in bucketfuls. He was sick of baseball. He was sick of everybody asking questions about Kirby. He would rather be home, watching his ants work in their ant-house, or catching grasshoppers for Manty, his praying mantis pet. Nobody would bother him then.

At last the field was cleared of players. The two base umpires walked out to their positions behind first and third. The plate umpire held his mask in one hand and announced the batteries: "Pitching for the Mustangs – Earl Lowe! Catching – Bill

Goff! For the Redbirds, Cappie Brennan is pitching — Dave Gessini, catching! Play ball!"

No sooner had the words left his lips than Jim Hurwitz nudged Bobby on the arm.

"Bobby, look!"

Bobby turned. His breath caught.

"Kirby!" he cried.

Kirby was coming around the corner of the dugout. He had on his cap and jersey, and he was carrying his mitt. He walked up to Coach Barrows. He said something and Coach Barrows looked at him in surprise. Then Coach Barrows cracked a wide, happy grin and gave Kirby a friendly tap on the shoulder.

"Thataboy, Kirby! I'm glad you came!" Bobby could just make out the coach's words above the tooting horns.

The Redbirds starting line-up was almost the same as it had been the other day. The only difference was that this time Tony batted ahead of Jerry Echols.

The team ran out to the field. Dave, with his chest protector and shin guards buckled on, caught three warm-up pitches from Cappie, then heaved the ball to second.

The Mustangs lead-off man took a called strike. Then he knocked a one-hop bounder to Cappie, who caught the ball and threw the runner out at first. The ball zipped around the horn.

"Way to go, Cappie!" Bobby shouted. He was smiling. He felt good. He was glad that Kirby had come. He wished that Kirby was playing. With Kirby on first base, Bobby would never have to worry how wild a peg he threw.

Kirby would stretch out his legs and arms as if they were made of rubber and *thut!* he'd have the ball.

A pop-up to Tony and a bouncing ball to Mark Donahue ended the top of the first inning.

Bobby received a rousing cheer as he stepped to the plate. *Smack!* The ball sailed over third base, curved and struck the ground in foul territory.

"Come on, Bobby!" a fan yelled. "Straighten 'em out!"

Bobby took a high pitch. Ball one.

Another pitch — high and wide. Ball two.

The red-headed southpaw for the Mustangs backed off the mound. He rubbed the ball in his hands and climbed to the mound again. He wound up, raised his right leg, and delivered. The ball came in like a white bullet. Bobby pulled back his bat and swung.

Crack! A line drive over short!

Bobby dropped his bat and scooted for first. He made his turn and raced for second. His cap and helmet fell off, but he kept going. He saw the center fielder pick up the ball. Bobby crossed second and headed for third. He ran hard, his sneakers kicking up dirt. He watched the third-base coach waving him on.

"Come on, come on, come on!" the coach kept yelling.

Bobby was a short distance away from the bag when he saw the ball bounce at his right. The Mustangs third baseman went after it. He caught the ball, started after Bobby with it.

"Hit it!" cried the coach.

Bobby slid toward the bag, just enough

out of reach of the third baseman, and hooked the bag with the toe of his sneakers.

"Safe!" yelled the umpire.

A triple! Bobby stood up and brushed himself off. His ears rang with the whooping cries of the fans and the blaring horns of the cars.

Al Dakin wiggled at the plate, and finally struck out. Bobby got nervous. After a hit like that, he wished that somebody would knock him in.

Toby Warren came through. He punched a single over second. Bobby scored. Jim Hurwitz flied out to left. The coach held Toby on first. Then Dave belted a grounder to short. Toby was running when Dave connected. The shortstop missed the ball, and Toby bolted for third.

The throw-in was wild and Toby scored.

Earl Lowe fanned Mark, ending the inning. The score was: Redbirds — 2, Mustangs — 0.

"I told you guys a couple of hits and Lowe would go to pieces," Jim said as he ran out across the diamond with Bobby and Al Dakin.

"Let's hope he stays that way," said Al, smiling.

Cappie threw six pitches to the first Mustangs batter and walked him. The next hitter bunted. Cappie raced in. He slid on the grass as he started to field the ball, and could not make the play.

Men on first and second. No outs. A good time for a double play, thought Bobby.

Crack! A grounder to second. Al Dakin came up with it, pivoted on his right foot, and threw the ball to Bobby. Bobby stepped on second for the put-out, and heaved the pill to first.

Too wide! Tony stretched, but he couldn't reach it! The ball bounced by, rolled toward the fence. The runner advanced to second. The runner who had been on second scored.

Bobby shook his head hopelessly. He was sure Kirby would have caught that ball. But why did he always throw so wild? The guys will really believe that I'm making Tony look poor on purpose, he thought unhappily.

"Come on, Bobby," said Jim from the outfield. "Throw 'em right, will you?"

Cappie mowed the next man down on strikes. The next Mustang popped out to Bobby.

In the dugout, Coach Barrows warned Bobby about his throws. "Take your time. Aim for Tony's head," he said.

Tony Mandos led off. He took a called strike, then a ball. Bobby watched Tony carefully. Here was the boy those officials were watching. Tony looked good at the plate. He stood with his feet apart, his knees bent slightly inward, his bat held off his shoulder. He had a nice build, too.

Crack! Up — up soared the ball like a tiny white meteor toward the outfield. The whole dugout emptied as the players swarmed out and watched the ball sail. Finally it curved down and disappeared over the center field fence.

Tony trotted around the bases. Once again Coach Barrows and the rest of the players surrounded Tony and shook his hand.

That was the only run the Redbirds scored that inning.

12

CAPPIE smiled as he warmed up with Dave. It was good to have a two-run lead.

The smile left his face immediately, though, after he threw the first pitch to the Mustangs lead-off hitter. The ball zoomed like a rocket between left and center fields. Both Toby and Jim raced after it.

Bobby's heart went cold. Toby and Jim were going to collide!

"Watch out!" he shouted. "Let Toby have it! Toby!"

Just as the ball was about to hit the ground, Toby reached out his glove, and caught it! Jim skimmed past him.

Bobby gulped. Boy! He thought they were going to hit for sure!

The next batter knocked a dribbler to short. Bobby charged in after it. I have to make this throw good, he thought. I must!

He reached for the ball. It took a bad hop, struck him on the knee. He leaped after it, picked it up, heaved it desperately to first.

Wild again!

Tony left the bag, stabbed at the ball with his mitt. He caught it, raced back to the bag. But the runner beat him to it.

Bobby turned around disgustedly. His throwing was wrecking the game.

Then Mark missed a grounder, followed by an error by right fielder Jerry Echols which gave the Mustangs two more runs. The score was tied now, 3–3.

"Let's settle down!" Coach Barrows shouted from the dugout. "Let's play ball out there!"

Man on third. A grounder to Bobby. He fielded the ball, pegged it to Dave, who was standing across home plate with his mask off. Dave caught the ball, put it on the runner.

"Out!" shouted the ump.

Bobby ran to cover second. Al was already there. Bobby took a deep, satisfied breath as he turned and headed for his position at short. He didn't know how he had done it, but that throw to Dave was perfect.

Cappie struck out the next Mustang hitter.

"We have that bad inning out of our system," said Coach Barrows. "Now, let's get in there and play baseball."

Al Dakin led off in the top of the third inning. He wiggled at the plate till a 2–2 count was on him, then cut hard and missed Earl Lowe's in-curve by six inches. Al sat down in the dust, facing the catcher with a very foolish look on his face.

Toby got on first by an error on the third baseman. Jim belted a fly to left that went foul, then drove one just inside the third-base sack. Toby circled to third, and Jim stopped on second for a double. Dave poled a long fly that went foul by an arm's length, then hit into a double play. They had lost a wonderful opportunity in gaining the lead.

The Mustangs came up and knocked two runs across before the Redbirds got them out. As Bobby expected, Coach Barrows made changes. He put Bert

Chase in Bobby's place, and Dick Carachi in Jim Hurwitz's place.

Mark fanned. Tony Mandos came up. Why doesn't Mr. Barrows replace him? Bobby thought sourly. Why doesn't he put in Kirby?

But this was only Tony's second raps. Maybe that was why.

Tony took a called strike. Then two balls. Then he blasted an inside pitch to left field that looked sure to be a hit. The Mustangs left fielder came in fast, caught the ball near his shoelaces. The fans for both teams cheered. That was one of the best catches of the year.

Jerry Echols walked. Cappie drove a hot liner through the pitcher's box, sending Jerry all around to third. But Bert, who had replaced Bobby, popped out to short. Three outs.

As Tony started for first, Mr. Barrows called to him. "Come back, Tony. Kirby's taking over at first. Nice game, boy."

Bobby wished that he was out there now. He could throw 'em anywhere with Kirby playing first.

Kirby caught a high peg from Mark, then made a put-out himself when he caught a fast-hopping grounder and stepped on the bag. He sure looked good — better than Tony, thought Bobby. The next Mustangs hitter went down swinging.

The Redbirds squeezed across a run in the bottom of the fifth. With two outs and two men on, Kirby came to the plate.

Hit it! Bobby whispered to himself. Hit it, Kirby! Those scouts were watching. Kirby *had* to hit.

Crack! A single through short! He *did* it!

Another run scored and the game was tied up again!

"All right, Kirby!" screamed Bobby, drumming his feet on the dugout floor. "You did it!"

The Mustangs held them scoreless the rest of the inning.

In the sixth, the Mustangs lead-off man singled. A bunt put him on second. Then a sharp drive through the pitcher's box scored the run and broke the tie.

The Redbirds tried hard to tie the score again, but the Mustangs held on to their lead like a hungry dog to a bone. They carried off the win, 6–5.

Every member of the team felt a little downcast. All except Bobby. He was not especially hurt. What he wanted to know was: Who would be picked on the All-Star team? Kirby or Tony?

That night he found out. The telephone rang at eight-thirty. Mrs. Jamison answered it.

"Bobby, it's for you," she said.

Bobby stared. "For me?" His hand shook nervously as he took the receiver from her. "Y-yes?" he stammered.

"Bobby? This is Curt Barrows. Got some nice news for you. You and Tony Mandos were selected to play in the All-Star game at Cooperstown. Congratulations!"

"*Me* and *Tony?*" Bobby's heart pounded.

"That's right. You and Tony. I've already told him. See you at the next game, kid."

Bobby hung up as if he were in a dream. He sat down, gasping for breath. He could hardly believe it. Me and Tony, he thought. Me and Tony.

But why wasn't it Kirby?

"Who was that?" asked Kirby. He was standing in the doorway.

"What are you so white for?" asked Ann. She was sitting in a chair across the room.

Bobby wet his lips. "Tony and I were picked on the All-Star team," he said, still half numb from the news.

A smile crossed Kirby's face from ear to ear. "Just what I figured," he said. "I knew you'd get it. I knew it all the time."

Bobby stared. "But you're the one who should have been picked! Not me or Tony!"

Kirby shook his head. "Not me. Tony's

a lot better ballplayer than I am. So are you. I had a hunch all the time that you and Tony would be picked. Guess I was right."

Bobby's eyes stung with tears. Kirby wasn't mad. He wasn't sad about it, either. He was taking it like – well, like a man!

Ann grinned. "Well, Mister Shortstop," she said, "how does it feel to be an All-Star player?"

"Fine, I guess," said Bobby. He thought about it a little more. The more he thought about it, the better he felt.

In a louder, happier voice he cried out, "Yes, sir! I guess I feel just fine!"

How many of these Matt Christopher sports classics have you read?

- ❑ Baseball Pals
- ❑ The Basket Counts
- ❑ Catch That Pass!
- ❑ Catcher with a Glass Arm
- ❑ Challenge at Second Base
- ❑ The Counterfeit Tackle
- ❑ The Diamond Champs
- ❑ Dirt Bike Racer
- ❑ Dirt Bike Runaway
- ❑ Face-Off
- ❑ Football Fugitive
- ❑ The Fox Steals Home
- ❑ The Great Quarterback Switch
- ❑ Hard Drive to Short
- ❑ The Hockey Machine
- ❑ Ice Magic
- ❑ Johnny Long Legs
- ❑ The Kid Who Only Hit Homers
- ❑ Little Lefty
- ❑ Long Shot for Paul
- ❑ Long Stretch at First Base
- ❑ Look Who's Playing First Base
- ❑ Miracle at the Plate
- ❑ No Arm in Left Field
- ❑ Red-Hot Hightops
- ❑ Return of the Home Run Kid
- ❑ Run, Billy, Run
- ❑ Shortstop from Tokyo
- ❑ Soccer Halfback
- ❑ The Submarine Pitch
- ❑ Supercharged Infield
- ❑ Tackle Without a Team
- ❑ Tight End
- ❑ Too Hot to Handle
- ❑ Touchdown for Tommy
- ❑ Tough to Tackle
- ❑ Wingman on Ice
- ❑ The Year Mom Won the Pennant

All available in paperback from Little, Brown and Company

Join the Matt Christopher Fan Club!

To become an official member of the Matt Christopher Fan Club, send a self-addressed, stamped legal-size envelope to:

Matt Christopher Fan Club
34 Beacon Street
Boston, MA 02108